'The kitten sat unde
holly bush. It was the
colour of black pepper and
mustard except for four
salt-white paws. Its fur
glistened as brightly as the
bottles in the Aunts' cellar
and over one eye it had a
black patch.

Ida knelt down before it.
"Why you look just like a
little pirate," she told the
kitten, "you must be a sea
cat!" '

But the Aunts don't want
a kitten and nothing Ida
said would make them
change their minds. It
seemed as though the tiny
kitten she had found would
have to stay out in the cold
and wet, unloved by
anyone . . .

BY MYSELF books are specially selected to be suitable for beginner readers. Other BY MYSELF books available from Young Corgi Books include:

MY GANG by Catherine Sefton
THE KILLER TADPOLE by Jacqueline Wilson
THE HAUNTING OF HEMLOCK HALL by Lance Salway
T.R. BEAR Series by Terrance Dicks
  ENTER T.R.
  T.R. GOES TO SCHOOL
  T.R.'S DAY OUT
URSULA CAMPING by Sheila Lavelle

Midnight Pirate

Diana Hendry

Illustrated by Janet Duchesne

MIDNIGHT PIRATE
A YOUNG CORGI BOOK 0 552 52417 4

Originally published in Great Britain in 1984 by
Julia MacRae Books

PRINTING HISTORY
Young Corgi edition published 1987
Reprinted 1987 (three times), 1988 (twice)

This book is set in 14/18 pt Century Schoolbook
by Colset Private Limited, Singapore.

Young Corgi Books are published by Transworld Publishers Ltd., 61-63 Uxbridge Road, Ealing, London W5 5SA, in Australia by Transworld Publishers (Australia) Pty. Ltd., 15-23 Helles Avenue, Moorebank, NSW 2170, and in New Zealand by Transworld Publishers (N.Z.) Ltd., Cnr. Moselle and Waipareira Avenues, Henderson, Auckland.

Made and printed in Great Britain by
The Guernsey Press Co. Ltd., Guernsey, Channel Islands.

Midnight Pirate

To Lesley
in your new room
love from
Mum & Dad
xx xx

1 About the Aunts

In November Ida was sent to stay with her two aunts, Aunt Madge and Aunt Dolly.

Both Aunts were fat. Aunt Madge was fat in the way of a wobbly jelly and Aunt Dolly was fat in the way of a fresh baked bun. They were both at least ninety and they had an old and ugly bulldog called Cleo.

The Aunts' house was thin and narrow and so cluttered with furniture and ornaments that Ida held her breath whenever Aunt Dolly steered her way, like a bus in traffic, round the hazards of tables and lamps and vases to Her Chair by the fire.

Aunt Dolly's chair was shaped to match her. It had important mahogany arms, a round wicker back and a

broad, leather-buttoned seat. Aunt Madge had a plain upright chair. Cleo didn't have a chair. She had a sofa draped with patchwork blankets because, as Aunt Dolly often said, 'We have to be very careful Cleo doesn't catch a chill.'

'Now where are you going to sit?' Aunt Madge asked Ida on the first evening after tea. 'Perhaps a cushion . . . or perhaps by Cleo . . . ?' Almost all of Aunt Madge's remarks began with 'perhaps' and ended in the air.

'She can have the small rocker,' said Aunt Dolly decidedly, and so the small rocker was brought from the kitchen and Ida, still in her best pinafore dress and white school socks, sat between her two aunts and Cleo and felt very miserable indeed.

All three of them slept and snored.

Aunt Madge went 'Hup! hup! hup!'

every minute or so.

Aunt Dolly's snore was a long under-water gurgle.

And Cleo's was a snort.

Ida made a face at Cleo and sighed a loud please-wake-up sigh. But the Aunts hupped and snorkelled on. And as the evening wore on and the sky grew darker and the street quiet, the month of November – all the thirty days of it which Ida was to spend in Coppermill with the Aunts while her parents were in America – stretched and stretched like a quite small piece of chewing gum will do when you grip one end with your teeth and pull and pull the other as far as your arm will go.

Rocking gently in the kitchen rocker Ida remembered her mother saying, 'Why, you'll have a lovely time darling! Aunt Dolly and Aunt Madge are perfect sweeties and their house is as cute as a doll's house.' As she spoke, Ida's mother was sweeping up the sand which every day blew into the front hall from the sea-front outside and managed to get everywhere as though it thought to turn the house into a beach.

Ida found she had a big ache of homesickness in her tummy. She tried to fold herself more quietly into the rocking chair. Five minutes passed, then ten. The snorers snored on. Cleo, dreaming of walks she used to walk, waved her paws in the air. Aunt Madge changed her 'Hup! hup! hup!' to 'Hip! hip! hip!' which came in squeaks from her nose. Very quietly Ida got up, crept out of the room and tiptoed up two flights of stairs to her small attic bedroom.

Her window looked out on a small garden in the middle of the square where the Aunts had their house.

Ida pulled the curtains and jumped into bed quickly. The house was too warm and too quiet. Ida longed for the familiar sound of the sea, the boomy winter sound or the splashy summer sound.

Who wanted a garden? Who wanted a clean shiny hall without a grain of sand to tell you of other worlds? Who wanted quiet when sea noises could tell of adventures?

Thirty days hath September, April, June and November, Ida said to herself. Thirty long and awful days with two fat Aunts and a pampered old bulldog and no-one of her own to love.

2 About Cleo's Terrible Nerves

In the morning Aunt Dolly gave Ida a large bowl of lumpy porridge.

'Porridge is good for children,' said Aunt Dolly. 'Makes them good and strong. Put salt on it child.'

'Well perhaps a little syrup might be . . . ' began Aunt Madge.

'Syrup on porridge is a sin,' said

Aunt Dolly.

Both Aunts were wearing aprons. Aunt Madge's striped apron seemed to have lost its ribbons and was pinned to her person. She had two big, clean dustbins before her and into these she tipped.

7 pints elderflower blossom
6¾ lbs sugar
1½ lbs raisins
3 lemons – rind and juice
and lots and lots and lots of cold tea.

And then Aunt Madge stirred, with a big wooden spoon, singing to herself as she did so, 'O Susannah, won't you marry me?' The tip of her nose had turned red with her efforts and Ida, nibbling tiny quantities of the foul porridge began to wonder if Aunt Madge were really a witch.

Aunt Dolly took a third tub and with a long plastic tube began filling

bottles with clear, sparkling liquid.

'Whatever are you doing?' cried Ida, pushing away her porridge bowl.

'Making elderflower wine,' said Aunt Dolly crisply.

'Making sunshine and rainbows,' said Aunt Madge gaily.

Beneath the kitchen table Cleo lay on a soft, powder blue blanket with a pillow for her head. Ida knelt down and tried to tickle Cleo's tummy. Cleo snarled.

'Cleo has terrible nerves,' said Aunt Dolly. 'She's so sensitive.'

'Perhaps I could take her for a walk this morning,' suggested Ida, for although she could not find it in her heart to *like* Cleo, she already felt as if she had been cooped up in this narrow, cluttered little house for two years not two days.

'A walk! In this cold weather? Why even in her tartan coat Cleo would catch a chill,' said Aunt Dolly.

'Perhaps round the garden?' murmured Aunt Madge, 'if the sun comes out . . . ?'

But the sun didn't come out and Ida spent the whole morning in the hot little house with her Aunts. Aunt Madge kept adding a log to the fire and Aunt Dolly kept checking that there was not a draught from door or window that could blow on the delicate Cleo.

All morning they filled bottles with elderflower wine and Ida was employed in carrying them down to the cellar where they glistened on the shelves. The cellar was cool and tidy. Jars of still-fermenting wine made a plopping noise like pebbles tossed in a pond. Large green apples rested on racks. A big jam pan hung from a hook. A net of elderflower hung from the ceiling to dry so that Ida thought the cellar looked like the flowery bower of a very practical fairy.

'Don't dawdle, Ida!' called Aunt Dolly and Ida had to run up the stairs for the next bottles.

In the afternoon both Aunts took a nap. Cleo, with the deep sigh of one from whom life asks just Too Much, staggered slowly from the kitchen to the living room and with an even greater effort, heaved herself up onto the sofa.

'There, there, my darling,' cooed

Aunt Dolly, tucking Cleo in with an extra pink baby's blanket, 'you have a nice sleepie byes.' Cleo rested her head on her paws and raised her sad eyes to the ceiling.

Aunt Madge, collecting a number of cushions, melted into them. Aunt Dolly lowered herself carefully into her wicker and leather chair, folded her hands in her lap and waited for sleep to fall from heaven.

And then her eye lit on Ida, who, truth to tell, she had, for the moment, forgotten.

Ida had found a pack of cards and sat on the rug playing patience.

Clearly she did not plan to sleep. It was very irritating. Aunt Dolly could see that Ida had found the Ace, King and Queen of Spades and the Ace and King of Diamonds, and the suspense of wondering whether the Jack of the former and the Queen of the latter would appear, kept Aunt Dolly from sleep. And then whenever she closed her eyes she was disturbed by Ida's pigtails in their bright red ribbons wagging to and fro like two metronomes keeping time for a very jolly tune.

There was something busy and not at all sleepy about Ida's figure sitting on the rug. Her sturdy legs made you think of running and jumping not of sleeping. Even Cleo seemed bothered, for she kept opening one gloomy eye to stare at Ida.

A distant memory came to Aunt

Dolly's mind about children needing fresh air and she sat up briskly and said, 'Put your hat and coat on child and go and play in the garden.'

Ida, well aware that she was being 'got rid of' put on her duffle coat and bobble hat, shut the door of the hot little house, crossed the street and went sulkily into the garden.

To a child who has had an endless beach for a playground, the garden in the square seemed a poor thing. It did not even boast a swing or a rubber tyre hanging from a tree. All it had was a bench that old ladies like Aunt

Dolly and Aunt Madge might care to sit upon.

But it was in the garden that Ida first saw the kitten.

3 About Some Very Fine Whiskers

The kitten sat under a holly bush. It was the colour of black pepper and mustard except for four salt-white paws. Its fur glistened as brightly as the bottles in the Aunts' cellar and over one eye it had a black patch.

Ida knelt down before it. 'Why you look just like a little pirate,' she told the kitten. 'You must be a sea cat!'

The kitten mewed and stood up, waving a fluffy tail that seemed several sizes too large for its body. It was so young that its legs wobbled when it walked. Ida laughed. 'You haven't got your land legs yet,' she said. The kitten sat down again and stared at Ida. Its eyes were as misty as a November sea, its nose like a knob of old soap. The kitten stuck this nose in the air and half closed its misty eyes as though it were thinking of great voyages across the ocean.

Ida reached out a hand and stroked the fur that shone like the holly leaves and flowered in a white ruff around the kitten's neck. Again the kitten moved away and this time Ida was reminded of someone who has put on ice skates for the first time. The kitten wobbled a few paws and stopped.

'Haven't you got a home?' cried Ida.

'Where's your mother and your brothers and your sisters?' The kitten mewed, wobbled back and rubbed itself against Ida's legs. 'You have very fine whiskers,' Ida told it. 'They must be at least three inches long and far too big for you at the moment.' The kitten purred at this compliment to its whiskers. 'Perhaps you'd like some milk,' suggested Ida. The kitten blinked and twitched its ears. 'If I knew where you lived I'd take you home,' said Ida. 'You're far too young to be straying in this way. I expect your mother is looking for you everywhere.'

The kitten gave a small, experimental miaow.

Ida looked all about her and the houses in the square, tall and silent, looked back at Ida. No face looked from a window searching for a small kitten – indeed Ida began to think that there was no-one behind those silent windows but sleeping Aunts.

'I shall get you some milk myself,' said Ida and she ran across the garden, through the gate, across the road to the Aunts' house. She had left the door on the latch and now it was easy to sneak in and creep down the hall to the kitchen.

From the living room she could hear the usual sounds.

'Hup! Hup! Hup!' – Aunt Madge.

'Snorkel! Snorkel! Snorkel!' – Aunt Dolly.

'Urgh! Urgh! Urgh!' – Cleo.

Ida took the milk from the fridge and set it on the table. What to put it in was more difficult. On the Aunts' dresser was an army of plates and cups and saucers but all of them of the finest china, gold rimmed and flowery. Ida did not think Aunt Dolly would be at all happy to think of a kitten drinking milk out of one of her best saucers. And then she spotted just the thing. One of Cleo's bowls!

Now most dogs have two bowls, one for food and one for water, but Cleo being Cleo (and the Aunts being the Aunts) had five. A big one for her dinner, a big one for her water, a medium size one for scraps, a small one for treats and rewards and a tiny

pink spotted bowl for her daily vitamin pills. It was perfect! Just small enough and shallow enough for an unsteady kitten. And secretly Ida thought it was quite pretty enough too.

She poured the milk into it and keeping one hand on top of the dish so that it wouldn't spill, she crept quietly out of the house, back across the road and into the garden where the kitten still waited.

Ida set the milk down on the grass. The kitten came carefully towards it, nose lowered, whiskers twitching. Then it crouched down and began to lap, its very pink little tongue rasping like sandpaper. Ida watched, her hands stuck in her pockets and a warm, happy feeling growing inside. As if the whole day felt the same way, a pale winter sun washed over the garden.

The kitten licked its long whiskers and looked up at Ida.

'I must go home now,' Ida told it, 'and you ought to go home too.' The kitten stared at her seeming to wink its one black-patch eye.

'I shall call you Pirate,' said Ida.

The kitten winked again.

Ida walked away across the garden. 'Go home, Pirate,' she called to the kitten who still sat neatly under the holly tree. 'If you have a home,' she added miserably.

4 About Nasty Pussums

Ida found both Aunts in a terrible pother.

'Oh Ida dear, a most awful thing has happened,' said Aunt Madge. Her hair had fallen out of its pins and strayed wildly everywhere.

Aunt Dolly, the tough and commanding Aunt Dolly, was weeping into a large mug of elderflower wine.

'Whatever is it?' cried Ida.

Aunt Dolly waved a large bottle of purple and blue striped vitamin pills at her. 'Cleo's dear little pink spotted bowl,' wailed Aunt Dolly. 'Someone has stolen it and she'll never take her medicine without,' and Aunt Dolly dripped tears into her elderflower.

Cleo, meanwhile, sat beside her looking remarkably healthy and possibly pleased.

‘Well I’m very sorry,’ said Ida, producing the pink and white bowl from behind her back, ‘but I borrowed it.’

‘Borrowed it!’ cried both Aunts together, but not in the same tone, for Aunt Madge said ‘borrowed it’ high up in the attic of her voice and Aunt Dolly said ‘borrowed it’ deep down in the cellar of hers.

‘Perhaps to play dollies’ tea parties . . . ’ suggested Aunt Madge.

‘Certainly not!’ said Ida. ‘You see there was a kitten . . . with such sweet long whiskers and a little white ruff and . . . ’

‘A kitten!’ said both Aunts in the same attic and cellar voices as before and as much surprised as if Ida had said there was a dodo or a pterodactyl.

‘Yes,’ said Ida. ‘I found him in the garden, wobbling about on such shaky little legs – he can’t be more

than a few weeks old.'

'You shouldn't speak to stray kittens,' said Aunt Dolly sternly.

'Well perhaps "hello" is all right,' said Aunt Madge hesitantly.

'No Madge, not even "hello",' said Aunt Dolly. 'Once you say hello to a stray cat it's yours for ever. It's like a mother, someone who will love you even when you don't want to be loved.'

'Well he seemed hungry,' said Ida, tossing her plaits in a defiant way, 'so

I got Cleo's bowl and I gave him some milk.'

'In Cleo's bowl!' cried Aunt Dolly. 'Cleo's very special medicine bowl that I bought at the antique shop?'

'It was just the right size!' said Ida. 'How was I to know it was so special?'

'O poor Cleo!' soothed Aunt Dolly. 'Did the nasty pussums have your very special bowl?'

Cleo let her head sag as though this was yet another blow of fate which she had to suffer.

'He is *not* a nasty pussums at all!' cried Ida bursting into tears, 'He is the sweetest little kitten I ever saw and much, much nicer than your fussy old Cleo!' And with this she slammed the kitchen door and ran upstairs to her attic bedroom.

Aunt Dolly and Aunt Madge and Cleo stood in the kitchen and shook in all their limbs.

Supper that evening was a very cold affair. Cold meat and cold feelings. Aunt Dolly clacked the salad spoons as though they were the snapping jaws of a crocodile. Even the salad cream fell in doleful dollops from the bottle. Just as they were finishing a lemon sorbet so icy that it made Ida's teeth ache, there came a small sound at the kitchen window.

'Mew, mew,' went the sound, then a scratch at the pane and 'mew, mew,' again. Aunt Dolly, Aunt Madge and Ida, all with a silver teaspoon of iced sorbet halfway to their mouths, froze.

Aunt Dolly put down her spoon, blew out her already large chest, strode to the window and without a word pulled down the blind.

'But it's Pirate!' cried Ida, jumping up. 'It has to be Pirate and he doesn't have a home and he's hungry!'

'No, Ida,' said Aunt Dolly sitting down again and chipping at her ice sorbet, 'we are not going to have anything to do with a stray kitten. He's probably got fleas. And think of poor Cleo's nerves, not to mention mine and your dear Aunt Madge's.'

'Perhaps a small saucer of milk . . . ' suggested Aunt Madge. 'He did sound like a particularly small kitten.'

'No Madge,' said Aunt Dolly. 'Ida should never have spoken to him in the first place. We have no room here for a kitten.'

It was a terrible evening. Aunt Dolly sat in her leather and wicker knitting a vest for Cleo, Aunt Madge sat in her upright embroidering a tea cosy. Ida sat on the rug between them doing a school project her teacher had set her while she was away from school. *The Cat Family* wrote Ida and underlined it with her ruler. 'In the cat family are lions, tigers, leopards and jaguars. There is also the wild cat and the domestic cat. The domestic cat came from Egypt.' Ida put down her

pen and began to draw a picture of the first Egyptian cat. Outside, in the cold English November night, Pirate the kitten mewed and mewed and mewed.

5 About a Midnight Pirate

Ida lay in bed and could not sleep. She heard Aunt Dolly bolting the front door and Aunt Madge bolting the back door and then both Aunts coming upstairs. Aunt Dolly's bed groaned twice, once for Aunt Dolly getting in and once for Aunt Dolly turning over. Aunt Madge's bed creaked and twanged for so long that Ida wondered if Aunt Madge was unable to sleep too.

She lay and listened to the distant sound of traffic and wished it was the sound of the sea. The house became silent. A church clock chimed twelve. A cold, sleety rain fell against the window pane. If Pirate was still outside he would be very cold.

Without her slippers Ida crept quietly downstairs – avoiding all the steps that creaked – and into the kitchen. Holding the blind by its small almond bobble she let it up very slowly. And there was Pirate, the sleet making his mustard and pepper coat look even glossier. He rubbed himself against the glass when Ida let up the blind and his small cries sounded tired and desperate.

The next part was even more difficult. It was a sash window that pushed up in noisy jerks. Ida edged it up until there was just a wide enough gap for her to reach out and lift Pirate in, holding him under his tummy.

She set him down on the floor. Pirate arched his back in fright and tried a few shaky steps on Aunt Madge's shiny tiles. Little paw marks began to appear everywhere. 'O dear,' said Ida, 'whatever am I to do with you Pirate?'

Pirate, spotting Cleo's five bowls ranged in a neat clean line, staggered across the kitchen to investigate and seemed to recognise the pink and white spotted bowl for he sat down before it and mewed.

'Well, I suppose I could wash it afterwards,' said Ida to herself. She fetched some milk from the fridge and poured it carefully into the bowl. Pirate lapped and lapped until it was all finished. 'You really are very hungry,' said Ida picking him up and holding him close. Through her night-dress she could feel his little body throbbing against her.

'I can't let you starve,' said Ida and she put the kitten down, opened the bread bin and cut a thin slice of bread. She broke it up into small pieces, poured on more milk and set it down before Pirate.

Again Pirate ate it all but this time, when he had finished he sat down and licked his paws and whiskers in the satisfied way in which a man in a fine

restaurant dabs his lips with his napkin. And then Pirate purred and purred and purred and the next moment curled himself into a croissant and seemed ready to go fast asleep.

'Oh Pirate, dear little Pirate,' whispered Ida, 'you can't stay here. The Aunts don't want a kitten and Cleo wouldn't like a kitten,' and shedding a few tears Ida edged open the window again and lifted Pirate out.

All the kitten's fur huffed with indignation and his tail wound about in spirals. He gave Ida one misty stare – as if to say 'Really! you are very rude' – then he jumped down from the window sill and disappeared across the road and into the garden.

Ida let down the blind, washed Cleo's bowl very carefully and crept back to bed. Whatever would the Aunts say if they knew they had had a pirate as a midnight visitor?

But Pirate wasn't the only visitor that night.

6 About a Different Pair of Whiskers

The next morning when Aunt Madge went down to the cellar for apples she heard a rustling in the net of elder-flower blossom. And then she saw a tail whisk through the apples and dis-appear into the darkness.

Aunt Madge gave a shriek, grabbed a handful of apples and came up the stairs as fast as her legs would let her. She twisted the key in the cellar door and stood there panting.

'Whatever is the matter with you?' asked Aunt Dolly, her hands and apron covered in flour from the pastry she was making for apple pie.

'Mice!' breathed Aunt Madge in a puffed-out whisper. 'Mice in our cellar!'

Aunt Dolly reached out for the apples and found the proof. Each had been nicely nibbled.

‘I’ve locked the door,’ said Aunt Madge shivering in her jelly flesh.

‘Don’t be so silly Madge,’ snapped Aunt Dolly. ‘Do you think mice are going to come and go through the door? Perhaps you expect them to ring the front door bell?’

‘All my elderflower blossom,’ sniffed Aunt Madge dabbing her eyes with her apron, ‘a whole summer’s blossom. I think they’ve made a nest in it.’

And while both Aunts stood staring at each other, a small brown creature – with whiskers of at least five inches – shot out of a hole by the cellar door, whizzed through Aunt Madge’s legs, missed Aunt Dolly by a hair’s breadth and fled behind the dresser.

Both Aunts shrieked. Aunt Madge climbed on the table. Aunt Dolly mounted the draining board by way of the kitchen stool and perched there, among the white breakfast cups and saucers, like an imposing stork standing on sea-shells. Cleo, moving faster than anyone had seen her move for years, dived into her basket and lay there trembling.

'I expect the mice have come in for the winter,' said Ida helpfully.

'The winter?' cried Aunt Madge. 'Oh dear me, I think they've come for ever!'

Aunt Dolly, still aloft the draining board and with her apron hauled up in case a mouse should try and follow her, found her most commanding voice.

'Where,' she asked, 'is the cat?'

There was a complete silence in the kitchen. Aunt Madge looked at Ida and Ida looked at Cleo and Cleo hid her head.

'W – W – W – What cat?' asked Aunt Madge timidly.

'Why *our* cat of course,' said Aunt Dolly. 'That little pepper and mustard creature who made such a nuisance of himself last night.'

'What makes you think he's ours?'

asked Aunt Madge.

'I've already told you,' said Aunt Dolly climbing down from the stool. 'Cats are like mothers. You don't choose them, they choose you. Ida, go and find him.'

With an enormous grin and with pigtails flying, Ida ran out of the house and into the garden. She looked under every bush and holly tree but there was no sign of Pirate. Ida called him by name and made odd pussy noises but still he did not come. Ida had to go sadly home and report to the Aunts that there was no sign of Pirate.

But secretly Pirate watched her from behind a dustbin.

Pirate was offended. He had not forgotten last night - invited in for supper and then, just when he was settling in, thrown out into the cold dark night. He would let Ida know that a cat was not a tame silly creature who would come when he was called, like a dog.

And so, only when he was good and ready did Pirate stroll - as well as he could on his wobbly legs - out from behind the dustbins, waving his over-large tail as if he was in no hurry at all for lunch, and jumped up onto the kitchen window sill where Ida had been waiting for him all morning.

'He's here!' cried Ida. 'Pirate's come!' And she pushed up the window and lifted him in. Pirate allowed himself to purr.

'About time too,' said Aunt Dolly regarding the small kitten now planted on the floor. 'In this house, Pirate, we have lunch at one o'clock precisely and perhaps you'll be kind enough to remember that in future.'

For answer Pirate rubbed himself against Aunt Dolly's legs and purred again. From the basket under the table came a groaning moan. Cleo, still recovering from the mouse, could not remember a worse morning since the vet had given her an injection in her bottom.

'Be quiet Cleo,' said Aunt Dolly. 'This is Pirate and you and Pirate are going to be very good friends.'

7 About Choosing a Home

And so Pirate the kitten moved into the house in the square with the Aunts. He did not catch any mice but he frightened them all away and Aunt Madge decided to hang her net of elderflower in the bedroom where she could keep an eye on it.

Cleo grew healthier and happier and

didn't need any more vitamin pills. This was because she spent a lot of time chasing Pirate up and down the stairs and the exercise was good for her.

Aunt Madge had a holiday from polishing the hall floor because during these chases Cleo skidded and, having no brakes, once went crashing into the front door.

Ida was happy because now she had someone of her own to love and to play with and Aunt Dolly was happy because Pirate chose her bed to sleep on and although Aunt Dolly did a great deal of 'tut tutting' about this, she was really very pleased.

December came all too quickly. Ida, with her bag packed and her coat on ready for the train, looked sadly out at the garden where she had first met Pirate. Aunt Madge and Aunt Dolly came down the stairs in their coats and hats. Aunt Madge had a big woolly bobble on her hat and Aunt Dolly three bright blue feathers on hers.

But Aunt Dolly was carrying a large wicker basket with a lid and a buckle at each side and the strange thing about this basket was that it went 'mew, mew, mew'.

'Here you are Ida,' said Aunt Dolly. 'It's been nearly as nice having Pirate to stay as it has been having you to stay, but I think Pirate belongs to you.'

'Oh Aunt Dolly!' cried Ida, knocking the blue feathers askew as she gave her Aunt a big kiss. 'Pirate chose your house. He should stay here.'

'No, it was you Pirate chose,' said Aunt Dolly, 'and you who fed him and you who loved him. So being a very sensible cat he decided that your home was his home.'

'But you will bring him to see us, won't you Ida?' said Aunt Madge peeping in the basket for a last look at Pirate.

'Of course I will,' said Ida.

So Pirate went home with Ida and there he became a proper sea cat for he walked on the beach every morning and ate shrimps for breakfast and slept in a sunny patch outside Ida's bedroom door.

And once a year Ida and Pirate went back to see the Aunts and Aunt Madge said they had never seen another mouse and Aunt Dolly said that Cleo had never needed another vitamin pill and they both said that

Ida and Pirate were growing beautifully.

But Cleo only snored!